For my mother, with love

Visit us on the Web! rhcbooks.com
Educators and librarians, for a variety of teaching tools, visit us at RHTeachersLibrarians.com

Library of Congress Cataloging-in-Publication Data is available upon request.
ISBN 978-0-525-64665-5 (hardcover)
ISBN 978-0-525-64666-2 (lib. bdg.)
ISBN 978-0-525-64667-9 (ebook)

The text of this book is set in 15-point Graham.
The illustrations were rendered in watercolor and pencil and assembled digitally.
Book design by Rachael Cole

MANUFACTURED IN CHINA
10 9 8 7 6 5 4 3 2 1
First Edition

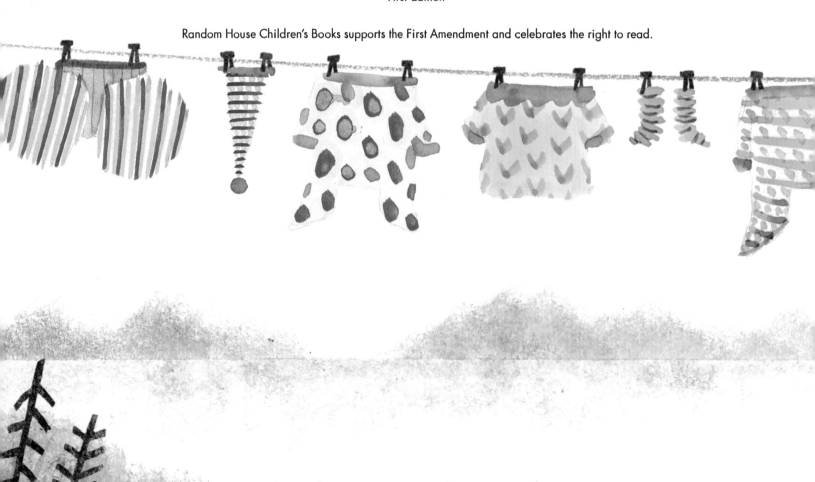

LAWRENCE
the bunny who wanted to be naked

vern kousky

schwartz & wade books · new york

E ver since Lawrence was a baby bunny, his mother has loved to dress him up in fancy outfits.

She always chooses the brightest colors

and all the most
interesting styles.

Sometimes she even invents new styles,

like sweater suits

and ear stockings

and
inflatable
helium
balloon
pants.

If it's just a tiny bit chilly,
Mrs. Rabbit wraps Lawrence
up in a snowsuit, two scarves,
and four furry winter hats.

And if it's warm out, she puts him in a protective swimsuit before he can play in the pond.

But Lawrence only wants to
hop naked through the fields.

"Every other beast gets to go naked. Why can't I?"

"Because," his mother always replies, "you are not every other beast. You are my one and only sweet little love-bunny."

And so day after day,
Lawrence forces his feet
inside of silly shoes

and hides his ears
under horrible hats

and tucks his
tummy into teeny
tiny yoga tights.

Mommy must be stopped! But how . . . ?

At last, Lawrence smiles.
And not a one-and-only-
sweet-little-love-bunny smile.

Late that night,
Lawrence cuts

and sews

and stitches.

The next morning, he gives his
mother a homemade gift.

"Why, Lawrence, you made me my own outfit! I love it so much I'm going to save it for a very special day."

"But," sniffs Lawrence, "isn't *today* a very special day?"

So Mrs. Rabbit wears her outfit when she drinks tea with the turtles

and when she shops for
the carrots for dinner

and even when she visits her
dear old friend Mr. Raccoon.

I love my little Lawrence, but thank goodness that's over.

Unfortunately for Mrs. Rabbit, it is nowhere near over.

You see, for Lawrence, there are so many other show-your-mother-how-very-much-you-love-her days.

There's Valentine's Day,

Mother's Day,

Mrs. Rabbit's birthday,

and especially Christmas Day.

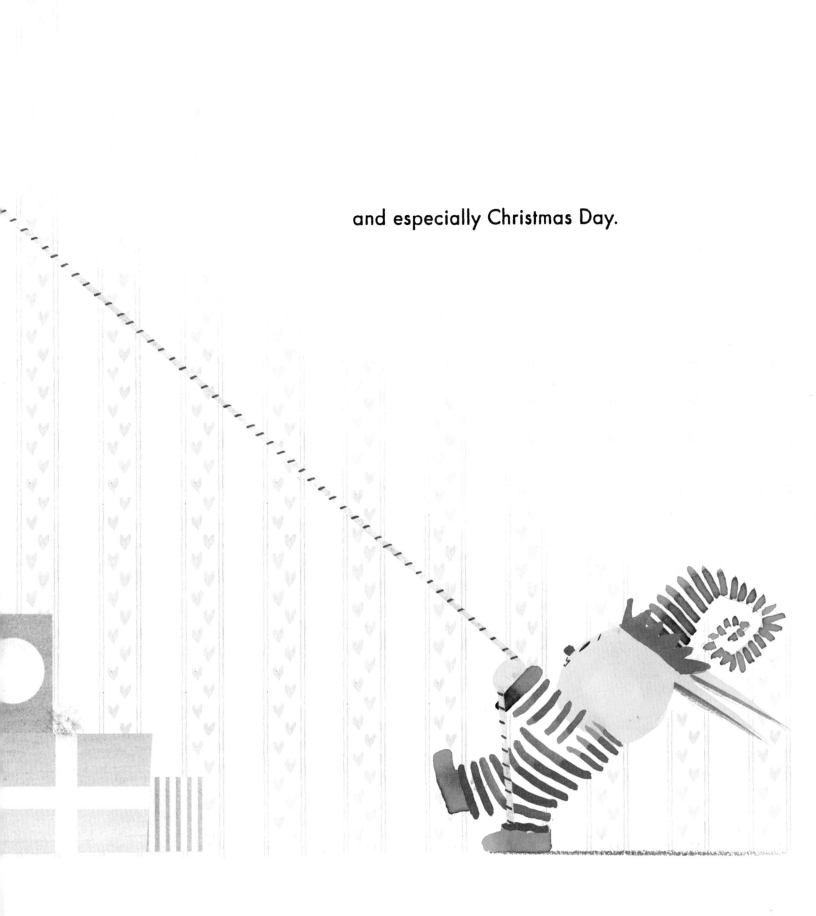

My goodness, worries Mrs. Rabbit. *Could this be how my darling Lawrence feels every single day?*

But then she smiles.

And for the first time, it's an I've-just-found-the-perfect-way-

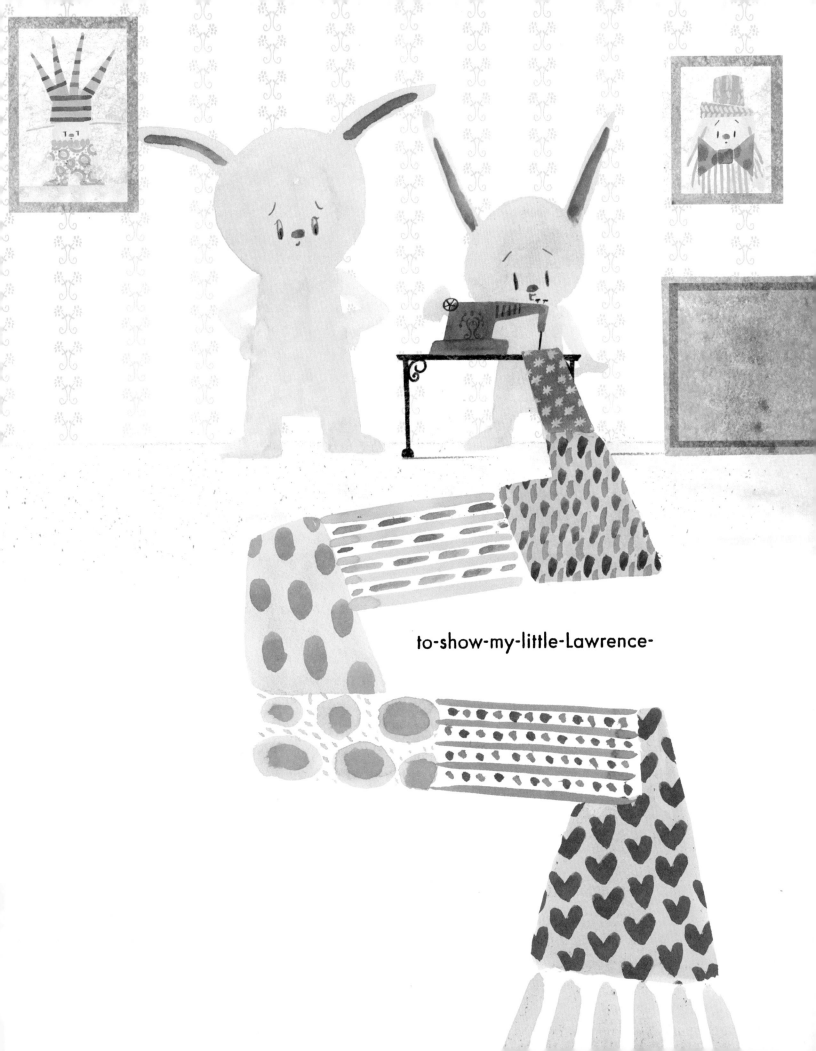

to-show-my-little-Lawrence-

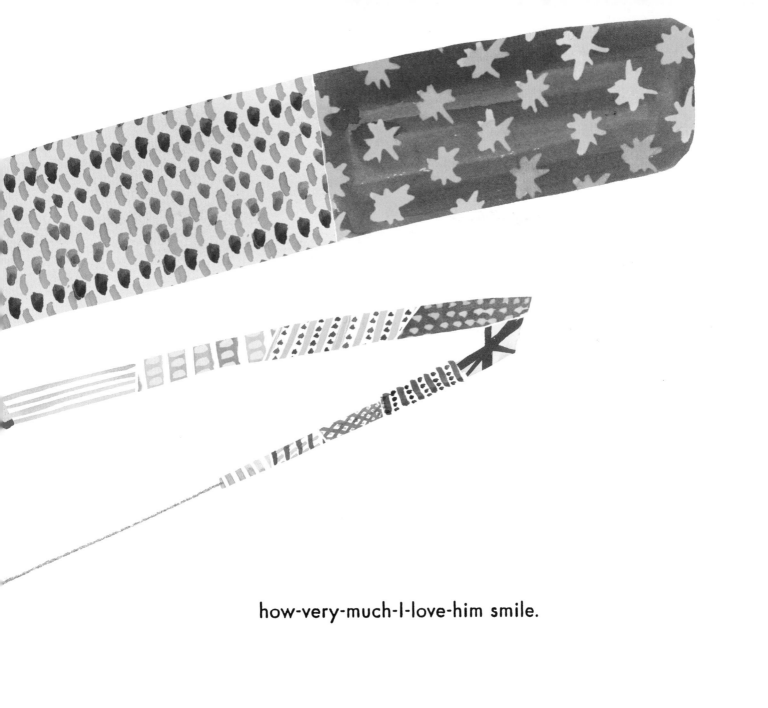

how-very-much-I-love-him smile.